KATIE MORAG'S
~RAINY DAY BOOK~

A Red Fox Book
Published by Random House Children's Books 20 Vauxhall Bridge Road, London SW1V 2SA
A division of The Random House Group Ltd

Copyright © Mairi Hedderwick 1999

1 3 5 7 9 10 8 6 4 2

First Published by The Bodley Head Children's Books 1999
Red Fox edition 2001
THE RANDOM HOUSE GROUP Limited Reg. No. 954009
www.randomhouse.co.uk

ISBN 0 09 940444 3

KATIE MORAG'S
~RAINY DAY BOOK~

Mairi Hedderwick

RED
FOX

A RAINY DAY POEM

Sometimes it can rain for days and days on the Isle of Struay. Although Katie Morag has the best umbrella and boots and puddles in the world, even she can get fed up with the weather and then she'll trudge into the house, slamming the door and dripping water all over the floor.

"Clean up those puddles!" scolds Mrs McColl. "It's a day for the ducks!"

"PUDDLEFEDUDDLE! UMBRELLAFALELLA! SMELLIEFUWELLIE!" shouts Katie Morag as she wipes up the mess. "SLOSHIEGALOSHIE!"

Katie Morag enjoys making up wet words. Do you?

Then Katie Morag writes a Rainy Day poem.

Puddlefeduddle, my pretty white duck,
Away to the shed from the rain and the muck.

"O no I will NOT, in the pond, I will wallow,
And beakfuls of worms I'll slurp up and swallow!

Puddlefeduddle, my filthy yuck duck,
All you can say is quacky quack quuck!

Fat with your dinner you sleep in the rain.
Puddlefeduddle! You're clean white again!

Rainbows are coming up over the Bay,
Maybe the sun will be shining today?

Puddlefeduddle, PLEASE hurry and fly;
We're off to the moor all sunny and DRY!

Why don't you write a rainy day poem too?

TIDELINE SEARCH

Grannie Island lives on the other side of the Bay.

Katie Morag often visits. It can rain there, too.

"What will I do," sighs Katie Morag, looking out of the rain spattered window. "There's nothing to do!"

"Stop moaning!" replies Grannie Island. "There's lots to do! Help me wash the baby clothes for your Mum... Make up your bed... Write a letter to Granma Mainland... Weed the potatoes... Tidy the sitting room... Feed the hens... Clean the hamster cage... Dry the dishes... Collect driftwood from the shore..."

What does she decide to do?

Katie Morag goes down to the shore. As well as driftwood, all sorts of other things have been washed up by the tide. There is something very unusual lying there. Can you find it? Why is it there? Has Katie Morag seen it?

SEASHORE

Mrs McColl won a prize on Show Day for her table lamp. She stuck sea shells in a pretty pattern round a glass bottle. She's going to give it to Neilly Beag for his birthday. Ssh! It's a secret!

Here are lamp bases you can make by filling bottles with sand, sea grass, pebbles or shells.

pickle jar

cider flagon

One of Mrs McColl's wine bottles

Katie Morag's jam jar

HOW TO MAKE THE SAND LAMP BASE: Wash beach sand in tap water to remove the sea salt and dry on newspaper. Divide varying amounts into 4 or 6 yoghurt tubs. Stir different coloured inks into each tub until moist. Leave to soak. Spread out each tub of sand separately on newspaper till bone dry. Return to tubs. Choose your bottle and make a funnel out of rolled paper to fit the bottle top. Pour different colours and amounts of sand in layers into the bottle to make stripes. You will need to get a DIY bottle lamp fitting. Until then put a cork into the bottle and DON'T SHAKE IT!

Just for fun, Katie Morag fills a jam jar with coloured layers of sand and then taps the lid to see how long it takes to mix the layers. How long do you think it will take?

PRESENTS

FLOATING DRAUGHTS BOARD

Use a waterproof black marker *polystyrene* *shell men*

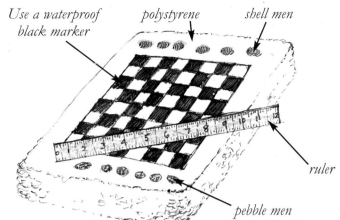

ruler

pebble men

PEBBLE PAPER WEIGHTS

Attach shells or tiny pebbles to large pebbles with strong glue. Decorate with acrylic paint. Varnish.

Mum

DRIFTWOOD GIFTS

GANNET WALL SCULPTURE

MIRROR

Glue a mirror tile and decorations onto trimmed driftwood or strong cardboard. Drill or criss-cross holes for creel rope hanger. Varnish the border if using seaweed. Why?

Seaweed hair will go damp when rain is coming.

PAINTED SNAKE

Cut off the side branches.

OUTDOOR MESSAGE PAD & WEATHER INDICATOR

Sorry we missed you!

SEASHELL CANDLES

You must have Grannie Island or another sensible adult to help.

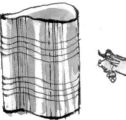   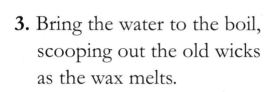

1. Squeeze an empty tin can (to give a pouring lip) and place in a pan half-filled with water.

2. Put candle remains into tin. (Cut off the charcoaled wick tips first.) Add a wax crayon to colour the white candle bits.

3. Bring the water to the boil, scooping out the old wicks as the wax melts.

4. Steady the shells for filling on crumpled pads of newspaper.

5. With oven gloves, SLOWLY pour the melted wax into each shell. Stop before the wax reaches the rim.

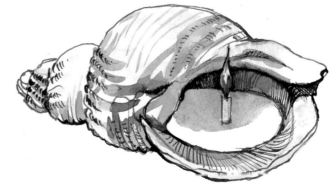

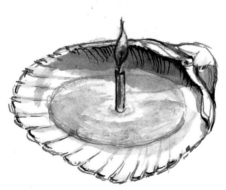

6. After 6-8 minutes, push birthday candles into the firming wax in each shell. If top-heavy, quickly pull the birthday candle out and cut off a bit at its base. Push back into the hole. WAIT until the Seashell Candles are COLD before lighting.

PICTURE LETTER WRITING

One day, Katie Morag received a letter from an admirer on the mainland. Look at how Katie Morag replied! She has done a PICTOGRAM - a picture letter. Can you read it? Could you write a picture letter?

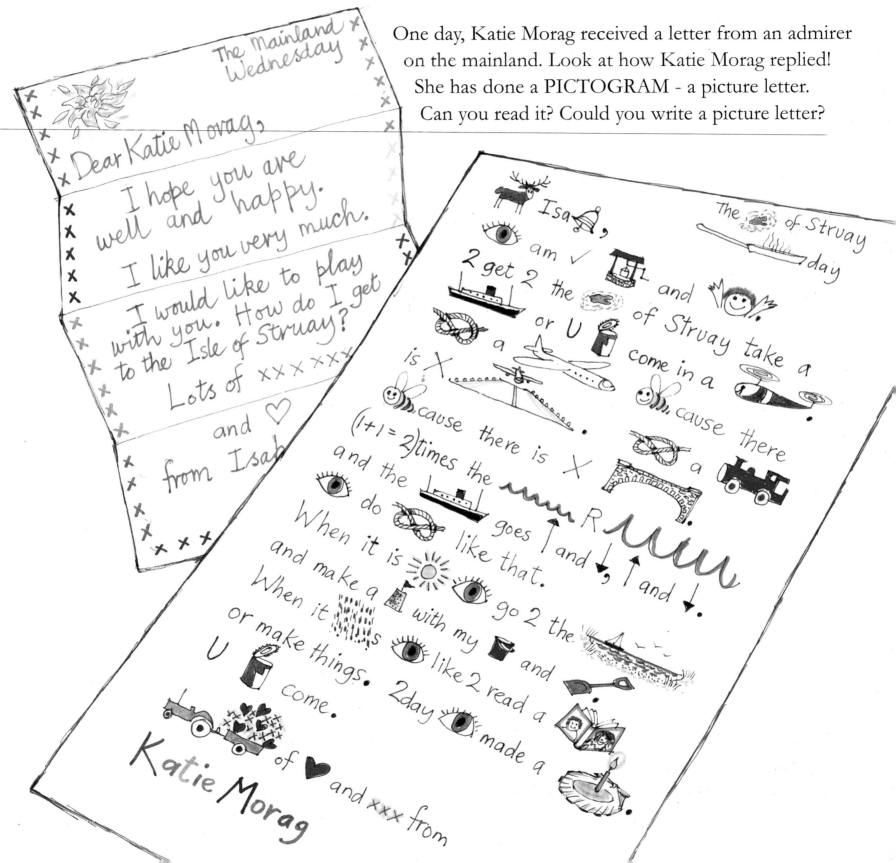

PUZZLES IN THE KITCHEN

It's Cosy and Comfortable in the McColl's kitchen. "I spy with my little eye," says Katie Morag, "something beginning with C." The Big Boy Cousins say there are HUNDREDS of things in the McColl kitchen that start with C.

"GEE WHILICKERS!" they say when they find out there are only 14!

How many words can you make from GEE WHILICKERS?
"HUNDREDS!" shout the Big Boy Cousins.
"A bit more than 14, I think,"
says Katie Morag.
"That's nearer the mark," say
Mr and Mrs McColl.
"Katie Morag usually
knows best," smiles
Grannie Island.

GARDEN IN A KITCHEN

Grannie Island loves making soup. She calls it BROTH. She uses lots of vegetables from her garden.

Katie Morag and Liam ask for the cut-off tops of the root vegetables and place each one in a saucer of water. Then they put the saucers on a warm windowsill. Why? In a few days, the tops will start to sprout.

Katie Morag and Liam have to make sure there is always water in the saucers. Why?

The tops grow and grow, and soon there is a garden INSIDE Grannie Island's kitchen!

CELERIAC

BEETROOT

PARSNIP

CARROT

TURNIP or SWEDE

A LOVEHEART CARD

Katie Morag has another grandmother who lives far away over the sea on the Mainland. She has just got married to Neilly Beag. He calls her a smart wee Bobby Dazzler!

Katie Morag is going to make Granma Mainland a beautiful lacy loveheart card!

Is there someone special you can make this card for? It doesn't have to be a Wedding Card, does it?

You'll need: A4 card, gold or silver paper doyleys, ribbon or lace, silver foil, glue, scissors, and anything you fancy for the fanciest of cards.

1. *Fold A4 card edge to edge and cut into 2 halves.*

2. *Fold the 2 halves edge to edge. You will have 2 cards. (Save one for later.)*

3. *Place large heart template on card at fold. Draw round. Cut out.*

4. *Fold doyley in half with gold side showing. The doyley must be taller than the card.*

5. *Flatten the card.*

   INSIDE

6. *Glue the gold side of the doyley onto the inside of the card with doyley frills showing at the top of the card, none at the bottom.*

    PLAIN SIDE OF DOYLEY

7. *Close card. More or less frills show depending on doyley size. Place medium heart template on gold heart at fold. Draw round and cut out.*

8. *Cut small heart from the cut-out medium heart. Glue small heart on front above large heart and leftover heart on top of card inside.*

9. *Make 2 small hearts out of aluminium foil and stick on front of card each side of large heart.*

10. *Glue lace, ribbon or cut strips of doyley along front sides and top edges - not the bottom edge. (Why not?)*

11. *Put the special person's initials on the right hand foil heart, yours on the left one, and an extra special message on the inside heart. In your best handwriting, of course!*

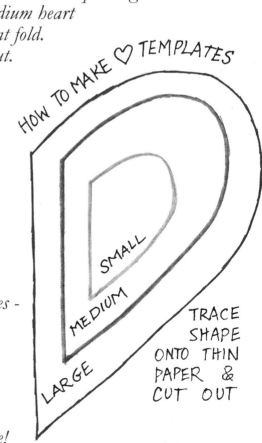

HOW TO MAKE ♡ TEMPLATES

SMALL
MEDIUM
LARGE

TRACE SHAPE ONTO THIN PAPER & CUT OUT

OLD AND NEW

SPOT THE DIFFERENCE

There are changes on the Isle of Struay.
Can you spot what is different about these
two scenes of the Village?
Katie Morag is in both of them.
Can you find her?

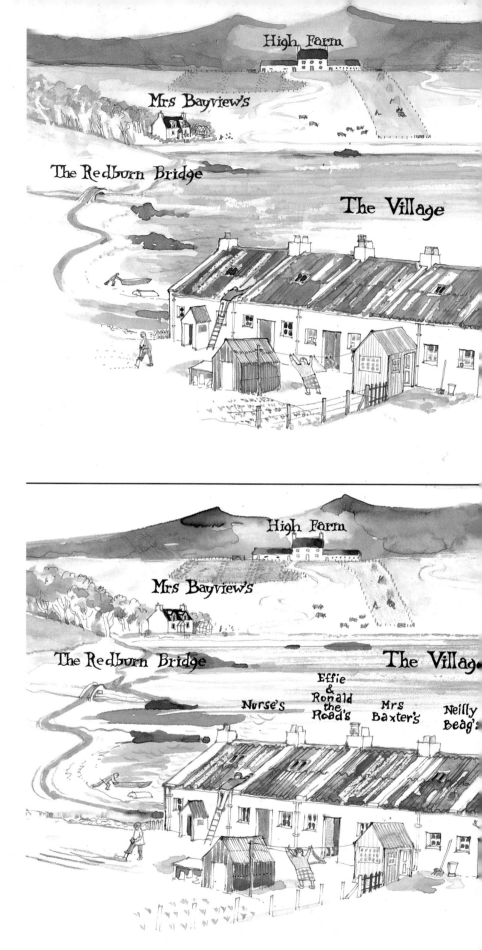

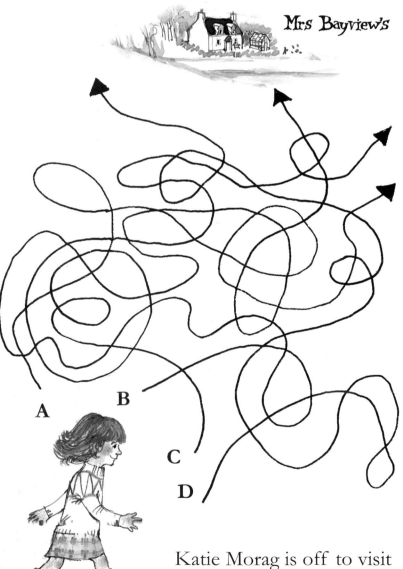

A   B

C

D

Katie Morag is off to visit
Mrs Bayview. Can you help
her find the best route?

THE ISLE of STRUAY

The Holiday House

The Lady Artist's

Grannie's

The Mainland

The Jetty

ISLE of STRUAY
SHOP & POST OFFICE

OBAN TIMES
GET YOUR COPY HERE

The Shop & Post Office

THE ISLE of STRUAY

The Holiday House

The Lady Artist's

Grannie's

The Mainland

The New Pier

The Ferryman's

The Jetty

TEAS

CRAFTS

TO THE NEW PIER

ISLE of STRUAY
SHOP & POST OFFICE

OBAN TIMES
GET YOUR COPY HERE

BISTRO

WELCOME

WEST HIGHLAND FREE PRESS

ORDER NOW

LITTER

KATIE MORAG'S FAMILY TREE

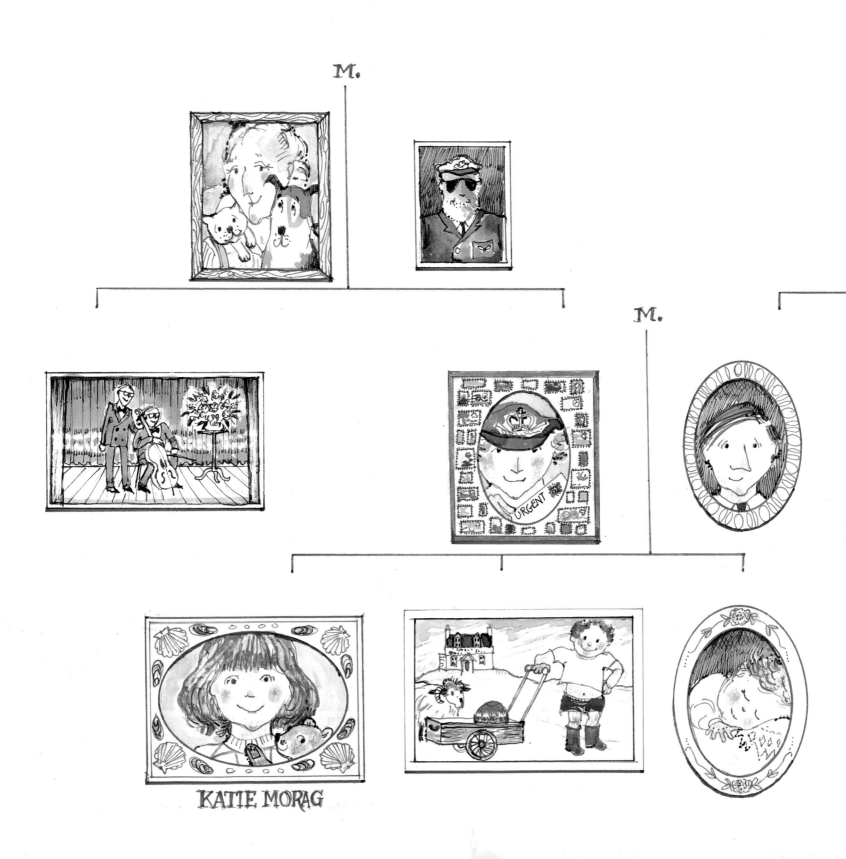

KATIE MORAG

This is the McColl Family Tree. Do you know who is who?
What would your family tree look like?

If you need some help, look in *The Big Katie Morag Storybook.*

BAKING DAY SECRET

Friday is baking day on the Isle of Struay. The best bakers on the island are the Ferryman's wife and Neilly Beag. Katie Morag always visits their houses in the Village every Friday afternoon. I wonder why?

NEILLY BEAG'S MERINGUE CATERPILLAR

BODY: Whites of 2 eggs, 100g (4oz) castor sugar, pinch of salt, green colouring

Whisk egg whites and salt until the bowl can be held upside down. (Careful!) Add a drop or more of green colouring. Fold in the castor sugar slowly. Put greaseproof paper on 2 oven trays. Place heaped teaspoonfuls of the mixture about 4cm (1½") apart on tray. Dust with castor sugar. Leave in the oven at 275°F, 140°C or Gas Mark 1 for about 1 hour - less if you want a gooey caterpillar inside, more if you prefer a crispy one. Turn off the oven, but leave the meringues in until they are completely cold. Ease off the tray with a palette knife.

JOINTS: 100g (4oz) butter or margarine. 125g (5oz) icing sugar. Lots of yellow colouring! Beat all together until smooth and creamy. Use smarties for eyes, nose and mouth, and cocktail sticks and smarties for the horns.

THE FERRYMAN'S WIFE'S CHOCOLATE CAKE

150g (6oz) butter or margarine, 150g (6oz) castor sugar, 3 level dessertspoonfuls golden syrup, $^1/_2$ teaspoon vanilla essence, 200g (8oz) self-raising flour, 40g ($1^1/_2$oz) cocoa, 3 eggs, a little milk.

Cream the butter or margarine, sugar, syrup, and essence until really creamy. Sieve the flour and cocoa. Beat the eggs well. Slowly stir the eggs into the butter mixture adding a little flour to stop curdling. Then fold in the remaining flour and cocoa. Add drops of milk until the mixture softly drops from a spoon. Put greased paper on the bottom of an 18cm (7") or 23cm (9") cake tin. Pour in the mixture and bake for $1^1/_2$ hours in centre of oven at 350°F, 180°C or Gas Mark 4.

TOP with chocolate spread.
DECORATE with toffee coated popcorn, or whatever you fancy!

SHOW DAY
SPOT THE DIFFERENCE

It is Show Day on the Isle of Struay.
The islanders are very busy preparing
the field for the arrival of the judges.
Everyone hopes their entry will win a prize.
Grannie Island has won the silver trophy
every year so far with her prize sheep, Alecina.
I wonder if she will win the trophy this year?
Katie Morag says she's going to make sure
Alecina does. Can you find Katie Morag
in each picture? And can you see all the
differences in each picture?
How many hours difference are there?

Can you help Katie
Morag find the best
way to her Grannie's?

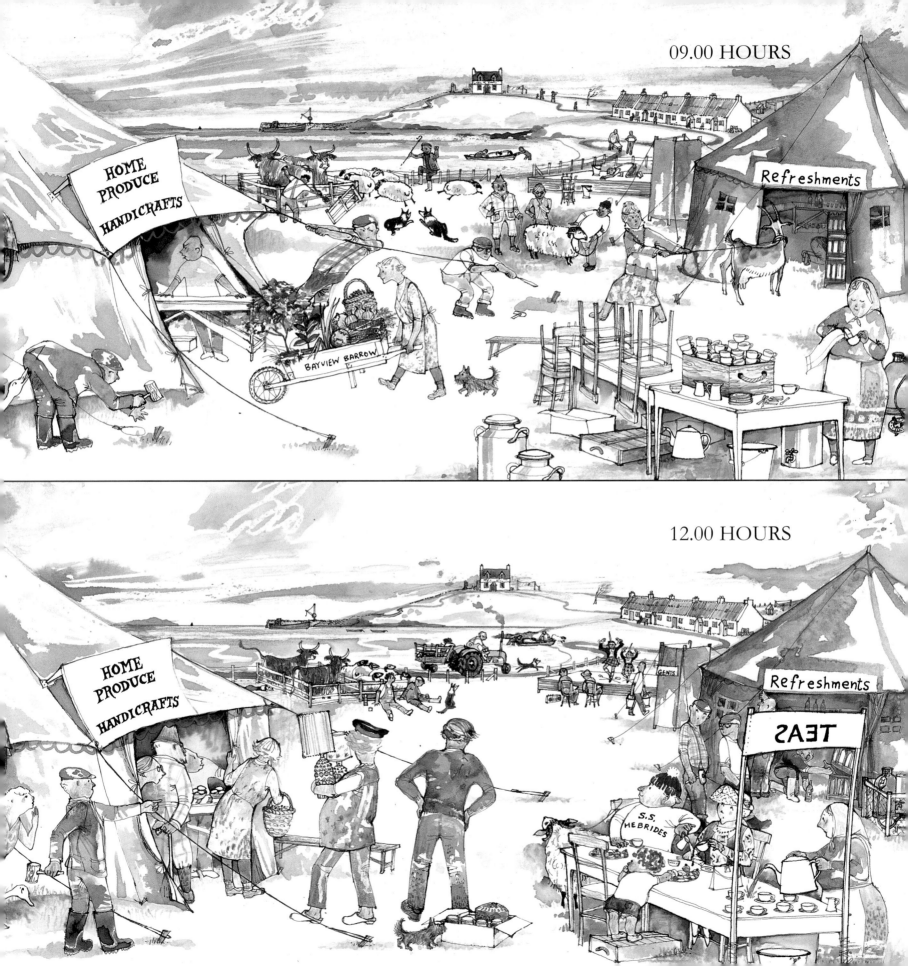

09.00 HOURS

HOME PRODUCE HANDICRAFTS

Refreshments

BAYVIEW BARROW

12.00 HOURS

HOME PRODUCE HANDICRAFTS

Refreshments

TEAS

S.S. HEBRIDES

GENTS

BIG EVENTS CALENDAR

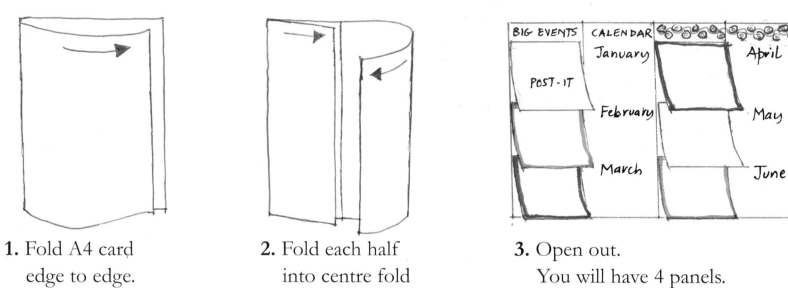

1. Fold A4 card edge to edge.

2. Fold each half into centre fold

3. Open out. You will have 4 panels.

4. Write BIG EVENTS CALENDAR along the top. Stick three Post-it notes, 76 x 76mm (3" x 3") in different colours if possible, on each alternate panel, as shown. Beside each Post-it note, write the months of the year, starting with January and ending with June. Draw pictures or patterns below the names of the months.

5. Turn the card over. Repeat the process but start with July and end with December.

6. On each month's Post-it note, you can write or illustrate the big event that happens to you. If there is more than one big event in a month, stick another Post-it note on top of the first one. Sometimes Katie Morag has six Post-it notes on the one month. I wonder which month?

7. Stand the calendar up by re-folding it like a concertina.

THE OTHER SIDE OF KATIE MORAG'S CALENDAR:

JULY: The Big Boy Cousins come on Holiday. I'm going to sleep in their tent!
AUGUST: Show Day. Help get Alecina ready for the Judges.
SEPTEMBER: Liam's Birthday. I delivered the Mail and fell in the burn.
OCTOBER: Hallowe'en. Liam always gets frightened. I WON'T.
NOVEMBER: Bonfire Night. Collect driftwood. Fry MOUNDS of sausages.
DECEMBER: XMAS!! A bicycle, PLEESE. Leave lots of chocolate for Santa.

High Farm

The Holiday H

The La

Mrs Bayview's

Bridge

31 32 33 34 35 36 37 38 39 40 41 42 43

30 29 28 27 26 25 24 23

17 18 19 20 21 22

16 15 14 13 12 11 10 9 8 7 6 5 4 3 2 1 START

Hall

School

The Village

Tearoom

Katie Morag has been asked to deliver the mail to the people who live on the other side of the Bay. She has lots of parcels.

DELIVER THE MAIL BOARD GAME

To play the game, you will need an egg cup, a dice and a wee button for each player. Each player will also need five counters which represent the five parcels in your mailbag. The winner is the first person to arrive at Grannie's house - without any parcels left. If you reach the end and still have some parcels left, you have to start back at the Post Office and go round again!

Ben Bog

The Boggie Loch

Artist's

Grannie's

44 45 46 47 48 49 50 FINISH

htie's Anchorage

Sound

Village Bay

Old Jetty

New Pier

Harbour Bar

(H)

The Shop & Post Office

Rag

MOVES

1 *Leave the Post Office with your mailbag.*

7 *Move forward 9 spaces.*

10 *Go back to the Post Office and tidy your bedroom!*

13 *Move forward 7 spaces and miss a go.*

20 *You've fallen in the water - mailbag and all! Quick! Pick up the parcels and miss a go!*

21 *You've fallen in the water - mailbag and all! Quick! Pick up the parcels and miss a go!*

22 *You've fallen in the water - mailbag and all! Quick! Pick up the parcels and miss a go!*

23 *Run forward 2 spaces to Mrs Bayview's. Give up a parcel.*

24 *Miss a go.*

25 *Drop a parcel on Mrs Bayview's doorstep.*

28 *Go back 3 spaces to Mrs Bayview's. Give up a parcel.*

29 *Miss a go.*

30 *Go forward 2 spaces to High Farm. Give up a parcel.*

32 *Fling a parcel on the High Farm doorstep. Run as fast as you can to 35.*

36 *Go back 4 spaces to High Farm. Give up a parcel.*

37 *Move forward 2 spaces to the Holiday House and give up a parcel.*

39 *Fling a parcel on the doorstep of the Holiday House. Run as fast as you can to 41.*

42 *Go back 3 spaces to the Holiday House. Give up a parcel.*

43 *Move forward 1 space to the Lady Artist's. Give up a parcel.*

44 *Fling a parcel on the Lady Artist's doorstep. Run as fast as you can to 46.*

48 *Go back 4 spaces to the Lady Artist's and give up a parcel.*

50 *You are at Grannie Island's! Give her a parcel - if you have any left.*
If you have delivered all the parcels - well done! Did Mrs Bayview, Mr McMaster at High Farm, the Holiday People and the Lady Artist get the right parcels? Read Katie Morag Delivers the Mail *to find out!*